This Walker book belongs to:

------------------------------

------------------------------

------------------------------

*For my wonderful sister Swapna, who is courageous,*
*beautiful and brilliant – all my love.*
S.P-H.


*To Katie, Benny and George.*
D.L.

*"Weeping may tarry for the night,*
*but joy comes with the morning."* – Psalm 30:5

First published 2020 by Walker Books Ltd
87 Vauxhall Walk, London SE11 5HJ

This edition published 2021

10 9 8 7 6 5 4

Text © 2020 Smriti Prasadam-Halls
Illustrations © 2020 David Litchfield

The right of Smriti Prasadam-Halls and David Litchfield to be identified
as the author and illustrator respectively of this work has been asserted
by them in accordance with the Copyright, Designs and Patents Act 1988

This book has been typeset in Bentham

Printed in China

British Library Cataloguing in Publication Data:
a catalogue record for this book is available from the British Library

ISBN 978-1-4063-9402-3

www.walker.co.uk

# RAIN BEFORE
# Rainbows

Smriti Halls

illustrated by

David Litchfield

WALKER BOOKS
AND SUBSIDIARIES
LONDON · BOSTON · SYDNEY · AUCKLAND

Rain before rainbows.

Clouds before sun.

Night before daybreak.

The old day is done.

There are mountains for climbing.

Journeys to take.

Dreams that are hopeful. Decisions to make.

Dark days may shake us. And worries creep in.

With dragons to duel. And battles to win.

Thunder will rumble, and lightning will flash.
The wind will start blowing, and tall waves will crash.

But ... there are footsteps to follow. And words that are wise.

A map that will guide us when troubles arise.

Friends who will help us, courageous and kind.

A rope to hold on to ...

and treasure to find.

Sowing and planting.

Roots before shoot.

Stem before flower.

Leaf before fruit.

Rain before rainbows, clouds before sun,
Night before daybreak, a new day's begun.

A day full of promise, a day full of light,

The morning is breaking ...

and the morning is bright.

# A note to the reader

## From the author:

There may be rain. But there are rainbows. I hope that this book and the beauty of David's illustrations can, in some small way, help us to acknowledge loss and sadness while giving voice to our strength and resilience. I hope it will remind us that there are friends to help us and new beginnings to be found. May it shine light in dark places and bring hope out of heartbreak – and may the promise of rainbows breathe through every page of this book, keeping us looking to the future with courage, light, and hearts filled with hope.

– Smriti Halls

## From the illustrator:

Drawing this book was a complete joy. As soon as I read Smriti's emotional, powerful words, I was inspired to capture that emotion in the pictures through the eyes of a little girl and her fox friend. They find themselves on a really tough and really scary journey, but they keep going, holding on to hope. One of my favourite messages this story illustrates is hope over fear.

– David Litchfield

*Rain Before Rainbows* sees internationally bestselling children's author Smriti Halls and Waterstone's Prize winning illustrator David Litchfield paired together for the very first time. Find out more about them online at smriti.co.uk and davidlitchfieldillustration.com.